Zatanna

and the HOUSE of SECRETS

Matthew Cody

AUTHOR

Yoshi Yoshitani

ARTIST

Ariana Maher

LETTERER

Zatanna

and the HOUSE of SECRETS

Zatanna created by Gardner Fox and Murphy Anderson

ZATANNA AND THE HOUSE OF SECRETS

DC Comics, 2900 West Alameda Ave.,
Burbank, CA 91505
Printed by LSC Communications, Crawfordsville, IN, USA. 1/10/20. First Printing.
ISBN: 978-1-4012-9070-2

PEFC Certified
This product is from sustainably managed forests and controlled sources
PEFC
PEFC/29-31-337
www.pefc.org

Library of Congress Cataloging-in-Publication Data

Names: Cody, Matthew, writer. | Yoshitani, Yoshi, artist. | Maher, Ariana, letterer.
Title: Zatanna and the house of secrets : a graphic novel / writer, Matthew Cody ; artist, Yoshi Yoshitani ; letterer, Ariana Maher.
Description: Burbank, CA : DC Comics, [2020] | Audience: Ages 8-12 | Audience: Grades 4-6 | Summary: Zatanna and her professional magician father live in a house full of magic, puzzles, and storybook creatures, but when she stands up to a bully in school, she returns home to find her father's gone missing within their own home.
Identifiers: LCCN 2019042101 (print) | LCCN 2019042102 (ebook) | ISBN 9781401290702 (paperback) | ISBN 9781779502049 (ebook)
Subjects: LCSH: Graphic novels. | CYAC: Graphic novels. | Magic--Fiction. | Fathers and daughters--Fiction. | Mystery and detective stories.
Classification: LCC PZ7.7.C626 Zat 2020 (print) | LCC PZ7.7.C626 (ebook) | DDC 741.5/973--dc23

TABLE of CONTENTS

Chapter One

There's a certain house on a certain street that everyone talks about.

A house full
of secrets...
prrrr
HISS

Eggs belong to the pan!
And pancakes and syrup are grand!

Seriously, Dad? It's way too early for Broadway breakfast songs.
They don't even make sense.

We're cooking fine, morning pancakes!
Fried *baaatter,* okay!
Do we have to let the rabbit on the kitchen table?
Pocus is getting straw everywhere.

You trick-or-treating tonight?
Dad, I'm a *little* old. Maybe Margo and I'll watch something scary.

You're all dressed up. Got a show?
Today, Zatara the Great will dazzle the good people of Shady Oaks Retirement Center!
RAEPPASID!
Okay, you can't slip a stack of pancakes up your sleeve, so where'd you hide them?
You should know by now, magicians never share their tricks.

Anyway, a senior center's not Broadway, but it's a gig.
You know, before she got sick your mom *dreamed* of making it to the big stage...
Anyone can do the big smoke-and-mirrors stuff but a magician who makes things disappear by speaking *backward* is...
Cheesy?
Epic.
You're going to blow the roof off the Shady Oaks Retirement Center.
COO-KOO!
I'm running late!

Wish you knew some *real* magic, Dad.
What I'd give for a spell to skip middle school.
Hello, Zatanna.
Late again?
Hey, Benji.
Where're you headed?
Art museum day.
Lucky.
I'm kinda sick of it.
Um, did you see the film center's doing a Jimmy Stewart festival?
Oh yeah? He's my favorite actor from, like, the *way-back* days.
We should go sometime.

Really?
Yeah, let's see a movie together.
That would be awesome!
Fun! Catch you later!
Hey, Homeschool! You allowed outside without your mom?
Why don't you leave Benji alone?
Zee, just let it go, okay?
Benji's rubber and you're glue! Whatever you say bounces off him and sticks to you!
C'mon he's just goofing around.
Plus, you sound like a sixth grader.

Margo, what are you doing?
Is that *makeup?*
What's the big deal? You want some?
Since when did you start wearing makeup?
Lighten up. Maybe you could use a little to impress Homeschool.
DANCE TONIGHT
His name's *Benji!* And all we do is talk about old movies.
Yeah, but you two talk a lot. People **see** you two talk a lot.

Hey, Margo.
See you at the Fun Night tonight?
I wouldn't miss it! See you there.
So now you're wearing makeup *and* you're going on a date with *Derek Winters?*
It's *not* a date.
It's the Halloween Fun Night! It's a *group* of us going.
Funny, *I* wasn't invited.
I was going to mention it...
Really, it was a last-minute thing. I don't even have a costume yet.
Forget it.
Seriously. Why *don't* you come? It would be fun.
RING!
Look, I can't be late for math.
And you've got straw in your hair.

RING! RING!
So I said, "Where's your mommy, Home-school?"
What a jerk.
Ugh, he even smacks his gum like a cow chewing cud.
Gross.
Hey, Zatanna, drool much?

HAHAHAHAHA
Man, look at her blush!
I wasn't! I'm *not!*
Hey, I didn't know you cared, *Zatanna!*
Too bad you're such a freak.
Oh god, I'm just getting *redder* and *redder* and...
...RED DER!
POP!
AAHHHHH!
What... what the heck?

RINNNG!
Worst.
Day.
Ever.
Hey, Zatanna. I got the film fest schedule!
PUBLIC SCHOOLS
Huh? That's great, Benji...
Benji, I'm super busy. Maybe...maybe you should go to the movie without me.
Worst.
Friend.
Ever.

sigh
It's just not time. She's not nearly ready.
I know it's All Hallows Eve, but whoever they are, I can handle them.
Dad? I need to talk to you.
Something *really* weird happened at school today.
You in your workshop?

Zatanna!
Dad?! What the heck happened to you? Are you all right?
I had an accident in the workshop. It's fine.
Wait, where are you going? And who were you talking to—
I'm sorry, sweetheart, but I booked a last-minute gig tonight.
I'll need you to watch Pocus for me. He's under the weather.
Do *not* let Pocus out of your sight until I'm back.
SLAM
O... Okay.

And then the school nurse said it was probably some kind of allergic reaction, but what allergy turns people bright red!
It was *freaky.*
I was such a jerk to Benji today. Totally brushed him off.
All because Margo doesn't think I'm cool enough to hang with the cool kids.
Then I come home and Dad's looking like he went ten rounds with Killer Croc.
What's he hiding?
Bet Mom would've seen right through Dad's bogus story.
But I bet she was never a jerk to her friends either.
You know what? We're *done* moping!

C'mon, Pocus, old pal.
Time for a little detective work!
DAD
I don't know why Dad even bothers locking his workshop.
I was like eight years old the first time I learned this trick.
Don't give me that look.
Who do you think taught me how to do this? Daughter of a magician, remember?
CLICK

ZATARA & SINDELLA
MAGICIANS EXTRAORDINAIRE
Dad said he had an accident in here, but everything looks fine to me.
And who the heck was he talking to?

Mom was so beautiful, Pocus.
The thing is, I don't remember her like that. I only remember her being sick.
There was this snow globe she gave me. Like a winter castle.

"I used to pretend that she lived there, in that magical castle.
"That she hadn't really died at all.
Silly.
I wonder what happened to it?
That's weird. Dad never forgets his top hat when he's got a show.
I look ridiculous, don't I?
Hey, what's this?
Dad's secret pen pal or something?

What? This is a letter from Mom!
My dearest love,
Thank you for the latest news about our daughter.
I miss her so, but I know you are doing the best you can without me.
It's hard being a single fath
a teenage girl, but
doing a wonderful job
She called me a teenage girl?
Wait, she's... alive?

ZATANNA & SINDELLA
Why'd you tell me she was dead, Dad?
Why? All these years...
WHY DID YOU LIE TO ME?
There's a certain house on a certain street that everyone talks about...
MAGICIANS
But no one knows the truth!

Chapter Two

CRACK

What else has Dad lied to me about?
You've known him longer than I have, Pocus. Too bad you're just an old rabbit.
No offense.
ding!

MARGO
Fun Night starts at 8. U should come!
To heck with this!
I like to dance and stuff.
I think.

Oh, come on.
Move it, rabbit!
On second thought, I've got an idea.
You like dancing, Pocus?

C'mon, stop wriggling around so much! This has to beat hiding in a top hat, right?

By the way, poop in my backpack and our friendship is so over!

DANCE TONIGHT

THUMP
THUMP
Dancing girl coming through!
Oof, sorry! That's your foot!
My bad.

Zee!
Over here!
I'm so glad you made it!
Isn't this *awesome?*
It's like we're inside a disco ball.
Great costume. Mine was sorta last-minute.
Did you hear? Derek is *still* red as a tomato.
No one knows why either!
Yeah, it's a *tragedy*.

OMG isn't it, though? *Total* tragedy.
I dunno, red's, like, the hottest color this season.
Oh my god, did I just make a pun?
Hey, what's that in your bag?
Ah! It's alive! It's got rabies and pox and stuff!
No! It's my dad's rabbit!
He's harmless!

You brought Pocus?!
This is exactly the kind of stuff that makes me *crazy,* Zee!
But who cares—
I care.
It can't be us against the world. I just...
I just want to fit in.
What's his costume supposed to be? Prep school vampire?
Later, creepy staring kid.

CRACK
What the...
Ow! Calm down, it's only a blackout, people!
SHOVE
Hey!
Let go!

That's my dad's rabbit!
SNAP

Let's get as far away from that creepy bunny-napper as possible!
DANCE TONIGHT
Ugh, my backpack's gone.
And my bus pass was in it.
Looks like we're walking home, Poc—
Oh no! Your key collar! It must've come off in the fight.
Dad's gonna ground me for*ever*.

As soon as we get in I'll grab us towels and—
Wait, did we leave the front door open?
Dad, you home?

What.
The.
Heck?

You! You're a bunny-napper!
And who is this?
Not the Caretaker, but... his daughter, perhaps?
Eep!

Oh! Stay a while.
That's better. Now, where's your father, child?
I don't know!
Who... who are you?
I am the Witch Queen!
And now I hold the key to a house full of *secret* magic.
Magic that lasts *forever!*

WHAM
Let her go!
Ah, the Great *Zatara*. Last Caretaker of the *House of Secrets*.
I trust my goblins didn't tire you too much?

I always like to warm up before a big show.
EKOMS EB ENOG!
Oof!
D-dad?
Zatanna, take Pocus and get out of here!
Now!

ZAP
KCIRB LLAW RAEPPA!
KA-POW
You lose, magician.

By the rite of All Hallows, I *claim* this house!
Now, tell me how to find the secret to everlasting power.
Oh no.
You... you don't understand anything.
No one claims the House of Secrets. It claims you. And you... you're not up to the job!
Fool.

Let's see what happens... when the last Caretaker is no more!
No!
SMASH
You dare?
Oh boy.

RAEPPASID!
Well, kid, you really messed up.

Chapter Three

You... you can talk!
Yeah, it's a day full of surprises, huh?

What's going on? Where's Dad?
What happened to our house?
Looks like it's awakened.

Awakened? Houses can't sleep.
And rabbits can't talk, remember?
But Dad—

Your dad's too clever a magician to disappear himself for good.
I'm sure he's around here somewhere.
Dad's still in the house?
Yeah, but don't go running in—
Dad?
Dad?
No! Zatanna, you don't know what's behind that door!

Hey, hey!
We'll grind bones into salt to season our stew!
Don't overdo it. You'll make everything taste like bone!
GRIIIIIND
SNAP

Um...
...wrong kitchen.

SLAM
I tried to warn you. This is not the house you grew up in. Not anymore.
I'm not leaving without Dad.
He can take care of himself! Your dad's one of the most powerful magicians in the world.
Dad?
Dad makes pancakes disappear.
Only for his little girl.
Zatara the Great is Caretaker of the House of Secrets.
And that means something, kid.

"Some say the House of Secrets dates back to the beginning of time. It was the *First* house, capital 'F.'

"It was filled with ancient secrets. Dangerous ones.
"And as long as there has been a House, there has been a Caretaker to look after it."

"The Caretaker's main job has been to keep the House's secrets out of evil hands.
"To do that, your father disguised it. Put it into a magical slumber.
See, the House *dreamed* it was an ordinary house, and that's what it became.

So my dad isn't who I thought he was, and my house isn't really my house.
You're not really a rabbit, are you?
I'm a pooka. Animal spirit. Magician's familiar.
Pocus the *pooka?* Really?
I dunno. Guess your dad thought it was funny.
The spell that kept the house asleep and hidden was maintained by a powerful *artifact.*
A key that kept the magic locked up tight.
Lemme guess, a *golden* key?
Yep.

The key that the creepy witch boy stole off your collar? Because I took you out of the house.
So it *is* my fault.
Don't beat yourself up, kid.
We knew **something** was up this morning when Zatara got jumped by those goblins.
He fought 'em off but got a heck of a shiner.

I told your dad we needed to let you know what was going on.
But he said you were still too young to know the truth about magic.
You know how he gets.
Overprotective.

I'm still not leaving.
Look, your dad's got powerful friends on the outside. We can find help—
By then it might be too late!

Whoa! Whoa, you tried that, remember? You go around opening doors and you don't know what you'll find.
I might find Dad.
Or you might find the Witch Queen!
Zatanna, *stop!*
Pocus, you saw the shape he was in. He could barely stand!
I don't know why Dad lied about my mom.
I don't know where she is, or what's even true anymore.
But I know I can't just run away.
I hate humans.
Fine, we look for your dad, but if we're gonna do this we need some serious magical backup.
We need a magician on par with Zatara the Great!
Someone close by.
Sounds good!
Who?
Say something backward.

Wait... what? Oh, c'mon!
Too scared to try?
No!
Then do it. Start with something easy.
Nice and harmless.
This is *stupid,* but if it'll shut you up...
Nice and harmless, huh? Let's see... **W...**
O...
WONS.
There, you happy now?
No, you gotta *mean* it. Words are just noise if you don't mean it.
Try again.

"What does the word make you *feel?*"
WONS
I made it snow!

Hours later in the House of Secrets...
Okay, let me try...
ADOS.
Still nothing. What about...
E, T, A, L, O...
ETALOCOHC!

I give up!
We've been at this for *hours* and nothing's working.
I told you, just saying things backward isn't enough.

And how many steps *are* there in this place?
Wish I could just wave a wand and magic us there.
It makes sense to start our search at the top and work our way down.
And it doesn't matter if it's wands or spell books—magic's hard!
Yeah, but *backward talking?* Really?
Could be worse. Could be blood magic.
Wait, seriously?
I'm an old pooka, kid. I've seen things.
How old is old?
Well, you know the story of King Arthur and the Round Table?
Sure.
It was *triangle-shaped* before I talked him out of it.

I said, "Arthur, buddy"—
Pocus, I've seen this picture before.
Creepy fella. What of it?
Stay here!
I wanna check something.
What are you doing? Don't get too far ahead!
Zatanna!
I'm right here.
What? How'd you get behind me?

Because we're going in circles! It's impossible!
Zatanna, calm down. Don't do anything rash—
SRIATS DNE!
POP

CRRRACK
Look out!
Stop it! Undo the spell!

What—what do I say?
You told the stairs to end!
Reverse the spell!

I don't know how to reverse it!
I can't think...!
Oh no!

Aaaahhhhhh!

Chapter Four

Aaaahhhhhh!
Huh? Where am I?

RUSTLE
RUSTLE
P— Pocus? Is that you?
What's a *pocus?*
You! Bunny-napper!
You're Zatanna, aren't you?
My name's Klarion the Wit—

PUNCH

Ow! Why'd you hit me?

That hurt more than I expected.

You stole the key off my rabbit and let that awful witch into our home.
That *witch* is my mother!
And only *I* get to call her *awful.*
Where are we? Some kind of dungeon?
Technically it's an oubliette. See how the only door is way up there on the ceiling?
Just great.
My uncle Ezekiel could tell you everything about dungeons.
Maybe that was because Mother kept locking him up in them.

How'd you even end up in here?
Well, after my *tactical retreat,* I went looking for Teekl, my pet monster.
But I stumbled into that hole up there.
You?
I made the stairs disappear.
You made a whole staircase vanish? You must be a *powerful* witch!
I'm *not* a witch.
Then what are you?

Thirteen.
Still, I bet you have magic enough to find a way out of this prison.
Neither one of us wants to end up a skeleton.
I suppose I could try to conjure a ladder or something.
Fantastic idea!
Yeah? Meanwhile what'll *you* do?
I'll hold the ladder, of course!
Lemme think...
REDDAL RAEPPA!
POP

Well, it's a start.
Stay still!
You're stepping on me!

CREEEAK
I've got it! I've...
Whoa.
Zatanna! Over here!

Pocus! Thank goodness you're all right!
Yeah. I, uh, could use a hand.
I think I'll do this old school.
I don't have this magic thing down yet.
CLICK
What's he doing here?
Hello again, rabbit.
I couldn't just leave him locked up.
Why not?
A few decades in a cell might teach that kid some manners.

Oh, you're mad about the whole *key* thing?
I didn't know what would happen. I only came with mother to get out of witch-school for the day.
But since you're obviously upset, I'll just be on my way—
Oh no you don't. You're staying with us where we can keep an eye on you.
Fine, but what exactly are we doing here again?
We're looking for my dad.
C'mon, let's find the stairs.
Try not to make them vanish this time.
Easy as pigeon pie...

I don't know what all the fuss was about. These stairs seem perfectly ordinary.
The last ones were a lot meaner.

So, I guess we just search room by room for Dad...?
With a word of warning...
If you find the *Black Door,* Zatanna, don't open it. No matter what!

Why? What's behind the Black Door?
The Land of the Dead. It's the *final* exit from this place.
If your dad went through there...
What *are* you two talking about?
You know, if we find Zatara there's a good chance we'll run into the *Witch Queen* again, too.
Mother? Oh, she will be *very* cross.
The Witch Queen can have this whole stupid house for all I care!
I just want my dad back.

KER-KRASH
AHH!
Teek!!
There's my girl!
And you found my potion pouch?
purrrrr
Huh. I wasn't really scared.
Maybe you should be.

At least she fetches.
Pookas don't fetch.

A library?
Reading puts me to sleep.
Then you're reading the wrong books.

Dad's a total bookworm. Maybe he's around here?
Dad?
Dad?
RUSTLE
RUSTLE
Umm...?

Answer my riddle or go no farther!

SLAM
hisssssss
Uh-oh.

It's locked!
What did it say about riddles?
It's a sphinx!
They ask riddles. That's what they do.
Answer my riddle true, and I will grant you a boon!
Wait, a boon?
Like a favor?
Careful, Zatanna!

Will you show us where my dad is? Zatara, the...the Caretaker of this house.
First, answer my riddle true...
"My spine is stiff, my body pale, yet I'm always ready to tell my tale."
Beware! Answer wrong at your peril!

Okay, before we say anything, let's put our heads together—
Oh!
Oh! I know!
"My body pale, yet always ready to tell my tale."
The answer is... a chatty zombie!
When Mother dug up Great Uncle Leopold he wouldn't shut up about it.
So, do I get some sort of prize now, or...

Wrong answers must be punished!
SLASH!
Heck of a paper cut!

TRIP!
Oof!
Zatanna!
I'm all right! I just tripped on a...
Wait, that's it!

I've got to have a fire potion in here somewhere! Or a jar of moths...
Just keep it busy, Teekl. Good monster!
Wait!
I can answer the riddle!
HISSSSS!

Answer or be punished!

"My spine is stiff, my body pale, yet I'm always ready to tell my tale."
A **book.** The answer is a book.
Correct.
You know, "book" was my **second** guess.
Now will you show me where my dad is?
You answered true.
But you alone.

Heeeellp!

SLAM

WhoOOoaaa!

Chapter Five

RUMBLE
Your father is near, child. The *truth* is near. Choose the right door!
What door—
Wait, you're falling apart!
Nothing is as strong as it looks, child. Sometimes paper sphinxes are no match for raindrops...
And sometimes witches...
Are no match for little girls!

sigh

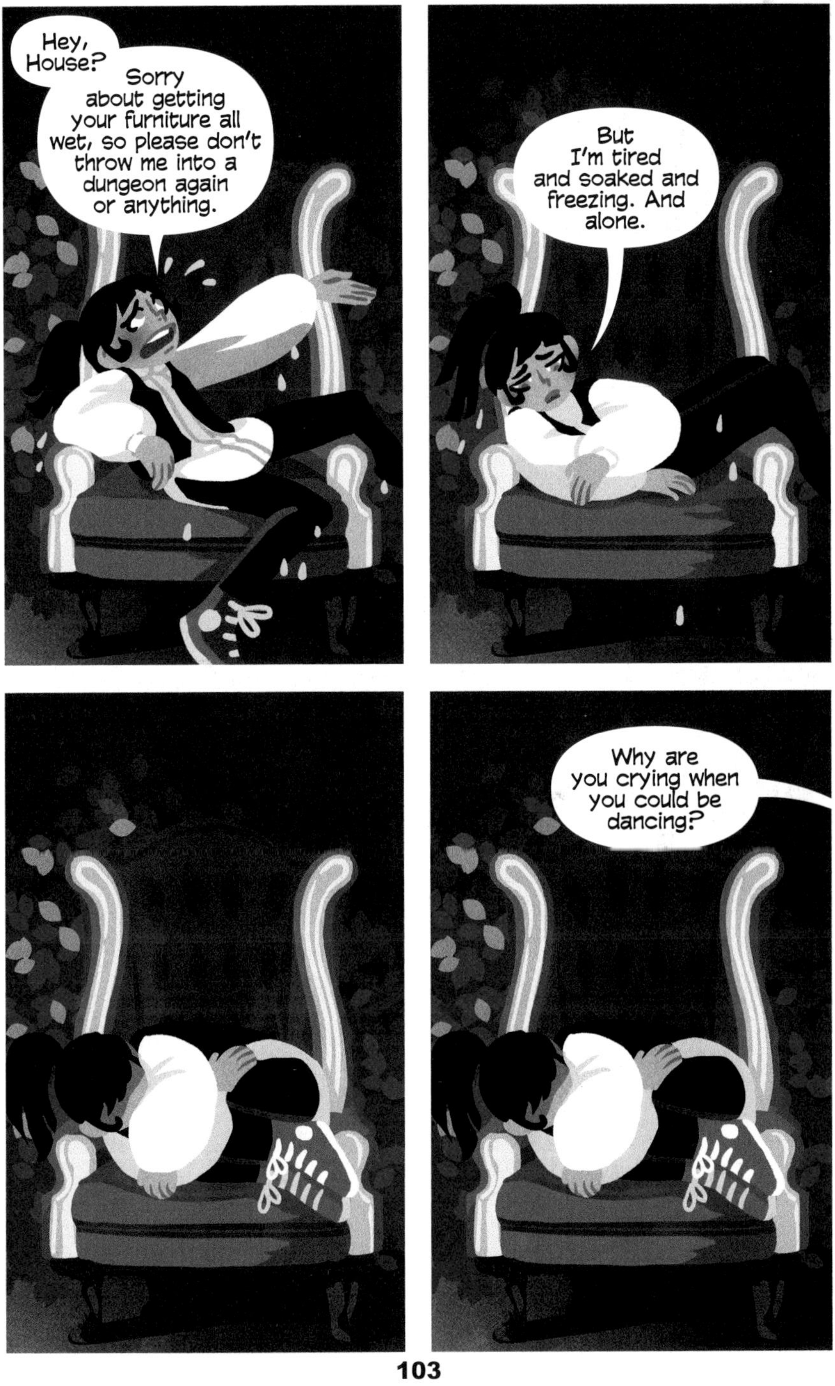
Hey, House?
Sorry about getting your furniture all wet, so please don't throw me into a dungeon again or anything.
But I'm tired and soaked and freezing. And alone.
Why are you crying when you could be dancing?

Wait, what?

Hi, Zee!
Hi, Zee.
Margo! Benji!
What are you doing here?
It's the Halloween Ball, silly.
Is *that* really the best mask you could come up with?
I'm...
I'm not wearing a mask.

We all wear masks!
Like the one you put on when your friends laugh at me behind my back.
I defended you! I told Derek that you were rubber and he's glue...
A nursery rhyme! What a *child*.
Hah hah hah
I'm not!
HA! HA! HA! HA! HA! HA! HA!
Stop it! Let go of me!

HA!
HA!
HA!
Ha!
HA!
Leave me alone!
Zatanna!
RIP!
Here!
Wake up!
SNIFF

What...what happened?
You were having a nightmare. Thrashing about, crying out.
You wouldn't wake up.

Lucky for you, the tincture of bullywug is so foul it'll break even the strongest slumber.
Wait, if I was asleep how'd my shirt get torn? Dreams can't hurt you.

Says who? Dreams are *deadly.*
Honestly, what do they teach you in human school?

Wait a minute— where's Pocus?
Oh, we split up to search for you.
I'm sure he'll be along soon.
Klarion, the sphinx said I needed to choose a door to find my father, but which one?
Each room is worse than the one before!
Couldn't someone else look for your father?
There's no one. My mom...
Well, I don't know where she is. Dad told me she was dead, but that was a *lie*.
I kind of hate him for that.

To be honest, if *my* mother disappeared I don't think I'd miss her that much.
You know, it's funny.
What is?
Here we are, risking our lives for people we don't really *like* all that much right now.

I have an idea. Let's use your magic to get out of here.
What?
I'd just mess up. I'm bad at this magic stuff.
Nonsense. You just aim too high, is all.
On the first day of witch school, you learn that sometimes a *little* magic is ***enough*** magic.
SNAP
Here! Try this.
A twig?
It's hazel! A witching rod!

Witch children use them to find things. Poison berries, moldy bones...
You know, cool stuff.
Here, use the rod to find us a safe way out of here.
Use your magic, but think small.
Fine. I'll try.
Dor...
DOR, DNIF DAAAAAD!
Whoa!
Dad? I thought we were leaving!

It's pointing this way! Dad must be...
Oh no.

Pocus warned me. He said the Black Door leads to the land of the...of the...
Dead.

No! It's not true!
Not my dad!
I'm sorry, Zatanna.
Maybe we should go.
Wait a minute.
WHIRRRR

It's turning!
Klarion, it's not pointing at the Black Door at all. That must be the one!
Wait!
Don't open it!
What? Why?
Because we don't need *them!*
Don't you see?
Without our parents we don't have to be the witch's son and the magician's daughter anymore!
We can just be *friends.*

That's silly. We already are friends!
Let's run away! We can go on adventures! We can—
Klarion, let go!
Help!
Help!
Hey, your pouch just talked.
Huh? No it didn't.
Zatanna!

I know that voice!
SUCOP, EB EERF!
POP!
PUFF
Pocus!
That kid and his mangy cat hit me with a shrinking potion when I wasn't looking.
The sneaky jerks.

How could you?
So I made him into a tiny rabbit in a jar. What's the big deal?
He's just like our parents! Always telling us what to do.
Don't follow us, Klarion. I don't want you around anymore.
What?
Wait!
You don't understand!
Zatanna, don't open that—

Hello again, child.

It's...my room!

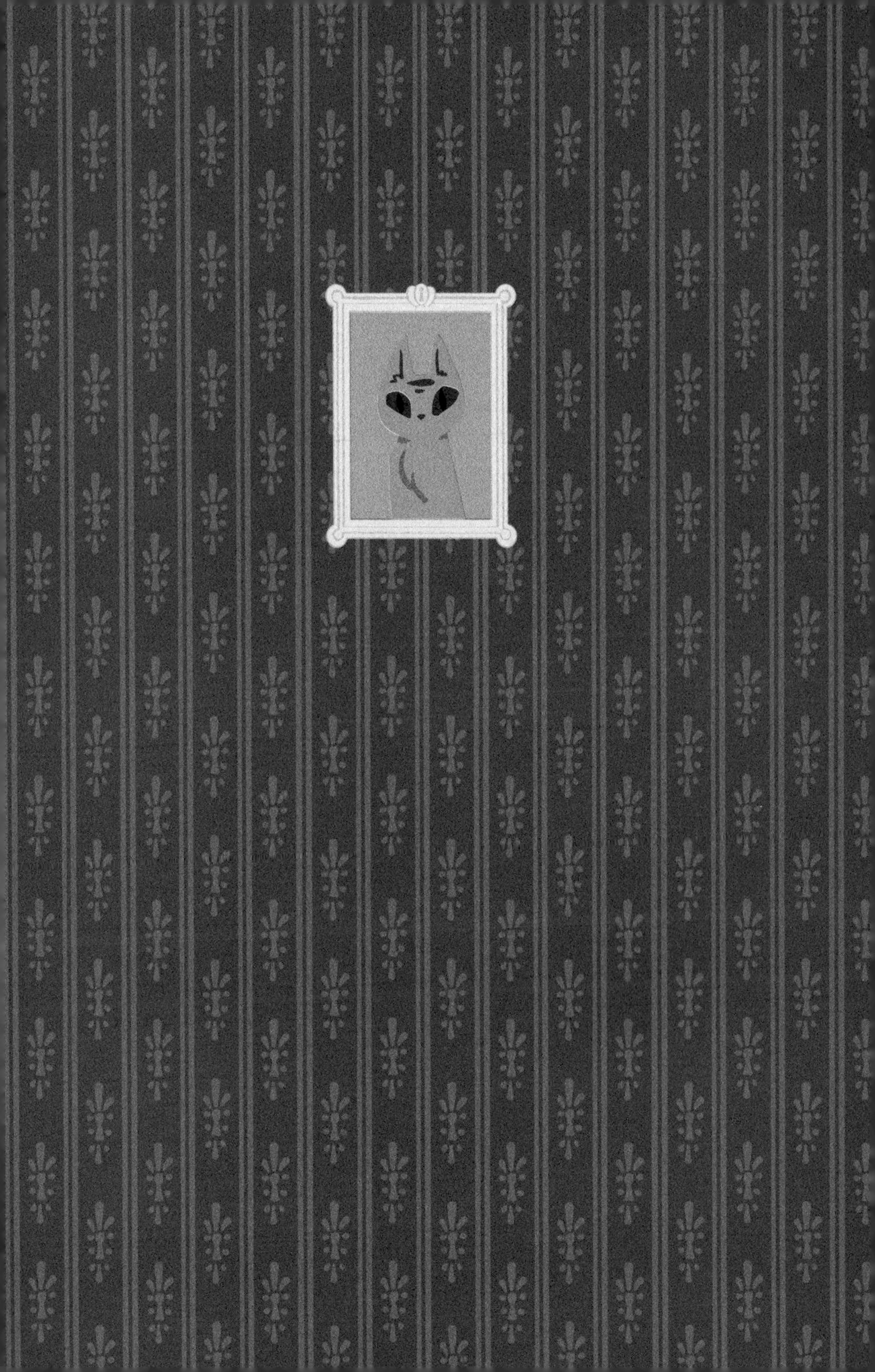

Chapter Six

Where's my dad?
Hee hee.
Gotcha!
Hey! Not the ears!
Speak so much as one backward *syllable...*
And the rabbit pays for it.

Now, child.
Someone's been waiting for you.

Dad!
Your father is my plaything now. A toy. But he doesn't have to stay that way...

Ah, Klarion!

You brought the magician's daughter to me just like I asked. Such a good boy.
Maybe I'll finally get you that pony.

Zatanna, I *could* release your father if you told me where to find the house's secret magic.
I...I don't know what you're talking about. Honest.

You are the last Caretaker's only child! Your father *must* have shared his secrets with you.
And you will share them with me!
Zatanna, run!
Help us, Teekl!
How *dare* you?
GROWL
That's my tiger! Get her, girl!

CHOMP!
YEOW!
Wait! What about Dad?
We can't help him if you're dead! Now run!
Where do we go?
Anywhere but here!

No, not the Black Door!
Eep!
Where do you think you're going?

No!
ZAP
POOF
Pocus!

There's a certain house on a certain street...
And inside that house is a door.
One we *all* must pass through in the end, but not too early!
H-hello?

For what waits beyond that Black Door?
Silence? Cold? The *uncaring* dark?
Please, anyone?
No, what waits there is...

Love.
Mom?

Imagine, dear reader, my surprise when my daughter walked through that door...
And told me the story I **share** with you now!
And then poor Pocus jumped in the way, and I fell through the door.
So...am I dead?
Only the true Caretaker can step through the Black Door and live, Zatanna.
Yeah, Pocus told me. But Dad's the...
Whoa.
"This house chooses its own Caretaker, and you were just a small child when it chose you!
"To protect you, we let everyone believe your father was the Caretaker. Even Pocus."

"But then I fell ill... and passed away.
"Your father began writing letters to me as a way of dealing with his grief.
"Imagine his surprise when I started writing him back!
"We exchanged letters under the Black Door for years.
I'm sorry we kept so many secrets from you, Zatanna. But parents make mistakes, even in the afterlife.
And your father needs you now more than ever.
But I'm scared, Mom.

I act brave but I'm really not.
That's *my* secret.
Secrets only hurt us if we keep them to ourselves.
Even in a house full of them.
As for the Witch Queen...
whisper whisper
Really? You think that would *work?*
There's powerful magic in being *who you are,* Zatanna.
The house chose you as its Caretaker.

"It's time for you to step into the spotlight!"
Why? I ended the line of Caretakers! Why won't this house share its secrets with me?

Maybe it's mad at you for being so horrible.

Careful! There's always room in my dungeon for one more, dear boy.

The secrets *will* be mine. I will tear this house down to its foundation if I have to!
No, you won't.

I don't believe it...

You wanted the last Caretaker? Well, I've been here all along.
How about *that* for a magic trick?
How...?
You were right—my parents did share a *secret magic* with me. I just didn't realize it.
They *loved* me.
You do know what love is, don't you?
Mother?

Lies! Now you presume to know the heart of the *Witch Queen!*
You are *nothing* but a child.
The only way to *save* your father is to defeat me...which means you've already lost!
This better work, Mom...
M'I REBBUR ERUOY EULG...
REVETAHW UOY YAS SECNUOB FFO EM...
ZAP

...DNA
SKCITS OT
UOY!
ZZZZ

NOOOO!

There's a certain house on a certain street...
WEEKS LATER.
I think it looks lovely on you.
Perfect for a first date.
For the last time, Mom, it's not a date! It's a group thing.
I gotta go. I'll be late.
Tell your father that I'm glad he and Pocus are back to normal.
And tell him I love him.

There you are!
Dinner's almost ready.
I'll grab a bite when I'm out. I'm late as it is.
I still think I should chaperone.

From Mom.
Thanks, kiddo.

KEOL, ROOD.
Looks like you're going out. Mind if I come along?
Actually, I do.
What are you doing here, Klarion?
Without Mom, the Witch Kingdom's in *total* chaos.
Technically, I'm next in line to rule, but I can't be ***bothered***.
So, I guess I should return her to normal someday...
Just not today!

Klarion, I have to go.
But it was good seeing you.
meow
Me too, Teekl.
Me too.
There's a certain house on a certain street that everyone talks about...
Hey, cool hat!
Thanks. Did you pick a movie?

But only you know the truth!
We thought we'd see whatever's playing.
We could just hang out and stay low-key. I mean, if that doesn't sound too boring.
A quiet day with friends? That sounds great.
In fact, it sounds like magic.
EHT DNE!

MATTHEW CODY

Matthew Cody is the acclaimed author of several popular children's books including the award-winning Supers of Noble's Green trilogy: *Powerless*, *Super*, and *Villainous*. He lives in Manhattan with his wife and son.

Photo by Alisha McKinney

YOSHI YOSHITANI

Yoshi Yoshitani is a California-based illustrator inspired by fairy tales and bright patterns. Yoshi uses their own multiethnic background to inform their work, creating bold graphic mythologies for the new mixed generation. Originally a concept artist for video games, Yoshi now freelances and creates band posters, book covers, and comics.

IT'S NOT SO EASY BEING A HERO— OR A VILLAIN!
WRITTEN BY KATE KARYUS QUINN & DEMITRIA LUNETTA
ANTI HERO
a graphic novel
ART BY MACA GIL
Turn the page to read a sneak peek of *Anti/Hero*, written by Kate Karyus Quinn and Demitria Lunetta, and illustrated by Maca Gil.

Welcome to East Gotham, the dark heart of the...
...suburbs.
Minnie, the ring is still here!
That's great, Sloane, but—
Call me Gray when I'm doing stuff for the Bear, Minnie.
Okay, Gray. But didn't the Bear ask you to create a big distraction?
I don't always have to do what he says.

Except that you kinda do?
Remember the part where he pays for all your tech toys? Like, um, me?
Don't worry, Minnie. I know what I'm doing.
The Bear will get his distraction when the police arrive to investigate the break-in...
And I'll pick up a few trinkets and treasures.

Meanwhile nearby...
Cheesy chips. The extra cheesy chips with CRUNCH!
CRUNCH!

Gotcha.
I don't think this belongs to you.
Better find out where it came from.
Oh my gosh, a robbery!
Now the **Hummingbird** gets to save the day!

CRUNCH!
CRASH!
BANG!
CRUNCH!
SMASH!
The worker drones are getting destroyed!
Sparky, it's up to you. Stinger on and beeline to the ring.
WEEOOO
WEEOOO
WEEOOO

Where do you think *you're* going?
Augh!
ZAP!
No way is a little robot bug beating me.
C'mon, Sparky... almost... there...
CRASH!

Come out with your hands up!
Drones! Time to buzz off!
These little guys are quick.
They're getting away!
Oh great. Yet another superhero's super mess.
Judging from that empty chip bag, it looks like the Cheesy Chipster struck again.
PAWN SHOP
Cheesy Chipster? I thought we were calling her the Wrecking Ball.

Back home...
I'm upgrading all the drones, Minnie. Next time we see that smash and crash clown—
Sloane, who are you talking to? Oh my goodness—
Cough
Cough
Cough
Did you find something for your robotics club?
Yeah... heh. You know how much I love the robotics club that's definitely a real thing at my school.
Sloane, I'm so proud of all the work you do—
Cough
—but even your amazing brain—
Cough
—occasionally needs rest. Lights out, okay?
Okay, Mom.

They called me the Cheesy Chipster.
And Wrecking Ball!
DONUTS!
Like I'm some sort of... *villain*.
I'll prove to them I'm a hero. No matter what it takes.
Continues in *Anti/Hero*. On sale April, 2020.